The Happy Hippopotami

The Happy Hippopotami

By **Bill Martin Jr** Illustrated by **Betsy Everitt**

Harcourt Brace Jovanovich, Publishers
San Diego   New York   London

HBJ

Text copyright © 1970 by Holt, Rinehart and Winston, Inc.
Illustrations copyright © 1991 by Betsy Everitt

Requests for permission to make copies of any part of the work should be mailed to:
Permissions Department, Harcourt Brace Jovanovich, Publishers, 8th Floor, Orlando, Florida 32887.

Library of Congress Cataloging-in-Publication Data
Martin, Bill, 1916–
The happy hippopotami/by Bill Martin Jr; illustrated by Betsy Everitt.
p.   cm.
Summary: The happy hippopotami enjoy a merry holiday at the beach, wearing
pretty beach pajamas, dancing the maypole, and battling with water guns.
ISBN 0-15-233380-0
ISBN 0-15-233382-7 (pbk.)
[1. Hippopotamus—Fiction. 2. Beaches—Fiction. 3. Stories in
rhyme.] I. Everitt, Betsy, ill. II. Title.
PZ8.3.M4113Hap   1991
[E]—dc20   90-37921

A B C D E
A B C D E (pbk.)

For Roger and Judy Bredahl
—B. M.

For Chris
—B. E.

Happy hippopotamuses
  Climb aboard the picnic buses
For a hippoholiday
  In the merry month of May.

BEACH

Happy hippopotami
  On the sunny beach do lie
Like a stretch of granite boulders
  Except, of course, for sunburned shoulders.

Happy hippopotamamas
  Wearing pretty beach pajamas
Spread tons of cheese on soda crackers
  To feed the hungry crackersnackers.

Happy hippopotapoppas
  Stroll about the candy shoppas
Giving children dimes and nickels
  To buy their favorite poppasicles.

Happy hippopotadaughters
Dive into the shallow waters
Splashing waves in stormy motion
Rocking ships across the ocean.

Happy hippopotasons
Fill their trusty water guns
And gallop out to squirt the foe
Like a cowboy picture show.

Happy hippopotapooses
  Toddling boldly on the looses
Stuff the pockets of their britches
  With gooey jelly sandywiches.

Happy hippopotamisses
  Dance the maypole, throwing kisses
To a crowd of gentlemen
  Who throw the kisses back again.

Happy hippopotamisters
    With hippy hair and hippy whiskers
Rock and roll their steel guitars
    Hoping they'll be TV stars.

Happy hippopotapilots
    Glide about in eagle flylets
Rising on the sudden breezes
    Whenever any hippo sneezes.

Happy hippopotamights
    Dressed in polka-dotted tights
Vie for hippopotaprizes
    Lifting weights ten times their sizes.

Happy hippopotamezes
    Fly about on high trapezes
Somersaulting through the air
    From way up here . . .

        to way down there.

Happy hippopotapreachers
   Call the hippos to the bleachers
For a ton of appreciation
   And another ton of inspiration.

At last the happypotamuses
Climb back aboard the picnic buses
With a "Hippo-ray! Hip-hippo cheer!
Until we meet again next year!"

The paintings in this book were done in gouache on Bristol kid finish paper.
The text type was set in Palatino by Thompson Type, San Diego, California.
Color separations were made by Bright Arts, Ltd., Singapore.
Printed and bound by South China Printing Co. Ltd., Hong Kong
Production supervision by Warren Wallerstein and Michele Green
Designed by Camilla Filancia